Just ~~o~~ ther
kitter
colo white
bits around his eyes and mouth. He tore
across the room, then jumped straight onto
the sofa, right next to Natasha.

"Oscar, what are you doing here?"
Siobhan laughed. "Oscar doesn't belong to
the same litter, as you can probably see
from his fur."

Oscar jumped up onto the back of the
sofa and peered down at Natasha. "Hello,
Oscar," she said softly, putting her hand up
to stroke his chin. Oscar started purring and
nuzzled his head into her hand.

"Oscar's only a couple of months old, but
he's already had an eventful life," Siobhan
told them. "He was a stray that someone
found sleeping outside a fish and chip shop."

Natasha thought about Oscar being on
his own and homeless, eating fish and chips
from a bin, and her heart melted.

# Have you read all these books in the
## Battersea Dogs & Cats Home series?

# OSCAR'S
## story

by
Sarah Hawkins

Illustrated by Artful Doodlers
Puzzle illustrations by Jason Chapman

**RED FOX**

BATTERSEA DOGS AND CATS HOME: OSCAR'S STORY
A RED FOX BOOK 978 1 849 41582 8

First published in Great Britain by Red Fox,
an imprint of Random House Children's Publishers UK
A Random House Group Company

This edition published 2012

1 3 5 7 9 10 8 6 4 2

The Random House Group Limited supports the Forest Stewardship Council
(FSC®), the leading international forest certification organization. Our books
carrying the FSC label are printed on FSC®-certified paper. FSC is the only
forest certification scheme endorsed by the leading environmental
organizations, including Greenpeace. Our paper procurement policy can be
found at www.randomhouse.co.uk/environment.

MIX
Paper from
responsible sources
FSC® C016897

Set in 13/20 Stone Informal

Red Fox Books are published by Random House Children's Publishers UK,
61–63 Uxbridge Road, London W5 5SA

www.**randomhousechildrens**.co.uk
www.**totallyrandombooks**.co.uk
www.**randomhouse**.co.uk

Addresses for companies within The Random House Group Limited
can be found at: www.randomhouse.co.uk/offices.htm

THE RANDOM HOUSE GROUP Limited Reg. No. 954009

A CIP catalogue record for this book is available from the British Library.

Printed and bound in Great Britain by
CPI Group (UK) Ltd, Croydon, CR0 4YY

**Turn to page 91 for lots
of information on
Battersea Dogs & Cats Home,
plus some cool activities!**

🐾 🐾 🐾 🐾

# Meet the stars of the Battersea Dogs & Cats Home series to date . . .

Bailey

Chester

Misty

Max

Daisy

Rusty

Snowy

Huey

Stella

# Playground Drama

"Not too high!" Natasha yelled.

"Don't be a baby, Tash," her big brother Jacob told her. "Libby's going higher than you."

Natasha saw her baby sister's face, pink with happiness, as she sailed up into the sky. "Wheeeee!" she squealed.

Natasha felt silly. Libby was only three and *she* wasn't scared of the swings. But

then Jacob pushed her hard again and
her stomach lurched.

"Stop it!" she
yelled. "I want to
get off!"

"OK!" Jacob
caught the
swing, bringing
it to a
juddering stop.
Natasha got
off, her knees
wobbly, and
Jacob picked up
his skateboard. As
the oldest, he was
meant to be in charge, but he was
more interested in doing skateboarding
tricks than looking after Libby.

Natasha watched until Libby's swing

slowed down, then she helped her baby
sister out and held her hand so she didn't
fall over. They walked towards the bench
where Mum was sitting. But as soon as
Natasha sat down, Libby ran off towards
the slide.

Natasha went to follow her, but Mum
put her arm around her. "Let her play,
she's fine," she smiled. Natasha snuggled
up to Mum and sighed again.

"Don't *you* want to play?" Mum asked.
Natasha looked at Jacob, who was
swinging on the monkey bars, his feet
dangling high up in the air, and shook
her head.

"Tash! Tash! Look!"
Libby called from the
top of the slide.

Natasha jumped
up. "Be careful,
Libby!" she called.

"She's fine, Tash,
don't worry so much,"
Mum said, waving at
Libby. Libby launched herself

down the slide so fast that
she shot off the end
and landed with a
bump on her
bottom.
Natasha gasped
and ran over to
her little sister,
but Libby just sat
up and laughed.

"Oops-a-daisy!" Mum said, coming over to pick her up. Libby climbed back up the steps for another go, and Natasha and Mum went back to their spot on the bench and watched.

Libby squealed as she slid down the slide over and over again, and Jacob gave a whoop as he stood at the top of the climbing frame.

Natasha started biting her fingernails. "Why does everyone think being adventurous is fun?" she grumbled.

"What do you mean, sweetheart?" Mum put her arm around her. "Are you all right? Did something happen at school?"

Natasha could only nod. She usually loved school. She was in Mrs Coveney's class, and she thought they had the nicest room of all. Mrs Coveney had put pictures of pretty yellow sunflowers all over the walls, and it was usually bright and quiet and cheerful.

But today when she had arrived everyone was noisily crowded around her friend Megan.

"Tash!" Megan had called when she saw her. "I'm having a birthday party, here's your invite." She'd handed her a pink envelope.

"It's in an adventure park!" Gavin had said excitedly. "There's a walkway really high up, and a zip wire so you can swing between the trees like Tarzan!"

All the boys in the class had started racing around doing Tarzan impressions.

"It's really fun, Tash," Megan had told
her. "My big brother had a party there
last year and Jacob came."

"Sounds great," Natasha had
mumbled weakly.

Now she rummaged in her schoolbag
and gave the envelope to
Mum. On the
front of the
invite was a girl
in a pink helmet
shrieking as she
swung on a rope.

Natasha's heart sank again as she
looked at it.

"Ah," Mum said as she saw it. "I can
see why you're a bit nervous. But
sweetheart, they won't make you do
anything you're scared of."

"I'm going to be scared of it *all*,"

Natasha sniffed. "I'm even scared of the swings!"

Mum gave her a hug and stroked her head. "You don't have to go if you don't want to."

"But Megan is one of my best friends – I *have* to go to her birthday party!" Natasha said, trying not to cry.

"If she's really a good friend then she'll understand," Mum told her.

"But everyone will be having fun without me!" Natasha looked at her feet sadly. "Why can't she just have a normal birthday party?"

# A Wonderful Surprise!

Mum's boyfriend Doug was already home from work when they got in. He looked at Natasha's sad face and ruffled her hair. "You look like you could do with some of Doug's special spaghetti bolognaise. Why don't you come and help me, Jacob?" he added, as he lifted Libby out of her buggy.

"Thanks, Doug." Mum smiled. "I'm

going to talk to Tash
about what we
decided the other
night. That ought
to cheer her up!"

Natasha looked
from Mum to
Doug in
confusion.
"What?" she asked.

"Come and sit down
and I'll tell you." Mum grinned.

Once she and Natasha were curled up
together on the sofa, Mum began. "You
know, Tash, everyone's different," she told
her. "Jacob and Libby are adventurous
like Daddy. He's got an exciting job in the
Navy, hasn't he? And you're a bit more
like me. The world would be a very
boring place if everybody was the same."

Natasha smiled at the idea that she was like Mum. But sometimes it felt like everyone else had all the fun. "I'm just a scaredy-cat," she sighed. "Everyone else is so brave and good at things and I'm not good at anything."

"Well, maybe you should try to be a bit less worried sometimes," Mum agreed. "But you *are* already good at something. In fact you're the best."

"Really?" Natasha said in amazement. "What?"

Mum reached over to give her a big kiss on her forehead. "You, my lovely Tasha, are the best at being caring," she said. "You're always looking after Libby, and making sure Jacob doesn't hurt himself. Caring about other people is one of the very best talents there is. I'm proud to have such a kind daughter."

Natasha felt herself
getting a bit pink as
Mum said nice
things about her.
She squirmed in
her seat.

Mum gave
her a squeeze.
"In fact, your
kindness is a
big part of a
decision that
Doug and I have
made. I know you and
Jacob have always wanted a pet . . ."

Natasha's heart started pounding so
hard she was sure Mum could hear it.
She'd asked for a pet lots of times, but
then Mum and Dad had got divorced and
they'd had to move house . . .

"I know it's all been a bit topsy-turvy the last couple of years," Mum said as if she was reading Natasha's mind. "But everything's settled now with us here, and Doug . . . so we were thinking . . . about getting a cat!"

Natasha threw her arms around her mother. "Oh thank you, oh thank you, oh thank you!" she cried.

"It'll be for everyone," Mum explained, her voice muffled by the hug. "But since you're bound to be the one who takes care of it, it'll mostly be yours. A real cat for my little scaredy-cat! We're going to a rescue home called Battersea Dogs & Cats Home. They have lots of animals all looking for a nice family."

Natasha didn't know what to say, so she just hugged Mum even tighter.

"Help! I'm being squashed to death!" Mum cried.

"So you've told her then?" Doug laughed as he came in. "These two are pretty excited as well!"

"Kitty! Kitty!" Libby chattered as she toddled into the room, Jacob right behind her.

"Woooo hooooo!" Jacob yelled, picking Libby up and swinging her around. Libby's feet knocked into the lamp next to the sofa, and Natasha had to dive to catch it before it fell to the floor and smashed.

"Whoa!" Mum said, taking Libby from Jacob and checking that she wasn't hurt. "You know, Tash, a little kitten is *almost* as troublesome as a little sister or a big brother."

"Don't worry, Mum," Natasha grinned. "I'm used to looking after troublemakers." Then she giggled and ducked as Libby and Jacob both launched themselves at her.

# Battersea Dogs & Cats Home

Natasha was squashed in the back of the car, in between Libby's booster seat and Jacob. Usually she hated long car journeys, but she was so excited she didn't mind Jacob counting all the red cars that passed them, or Libby singing *Incy Wincy Spider* over and over again.

When they finally arrived, Natasha looked up at Battersea Dogs & Cats

Home in surprise. It was hard to imagine
that inside that big building were lots of
cute cats and dogs!

While Doug and Jacob went on ahead,
Natasha and Mum held hands with Libby.

"Swing me!" Libby giggled. Mum and
Natasha swung their arms so Libby flew
up into the air between them. "Again!"
Libby shrieked.

"Come on, Libby, it's time to see the

cats now," Natasha told her. "There are lots in there, and one of them is mine, although he doesn't know it yet."

They walked into the reception and Natasha's tummy jumped with excitement. There were a few posters of cats in the waiting area, but no sign of any real ones. Mum and Doug gave their names to the receptionist and they sat down to wait. A minute later a smiling lady wearing a Battersea jumper appeared. "Hi, I'm Siobhan," she introduced herself.

Siobhan took them into a little interview room and asked them questions about their family and their house. "Jacob, Natasha and Libby go and visit their dad when he's home from the Navy, but I'm around all day with Libby during the week, so the cat wouldn't be on its own," Mum explained. "But it's going to be Natasha's pet really."

"Ooh," Siobhan turned to Natasha. "Are you excited?"

Natasha nodded eagerly. "I can't believe it!" she whispered to Siobhan, who laughed.

"Well, you should. There are so many cats up there who are desperate for a good home." Siobhan smiled at Mum and Doug. "We've got quite a few kittens at the moment too, so there are lots for you to choose from. Let's go up and see them."

They all followed Siobhan up a spiral staircase. The stairs led to a floor filled with little rooms with glass doors. In each one was a ladder leading up to a comfy

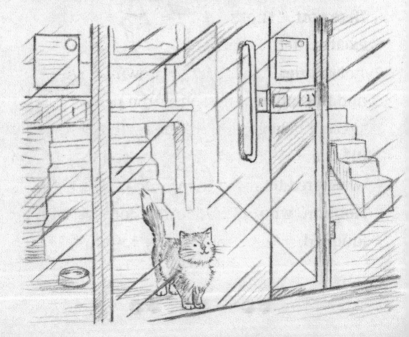

bed, some cat toys
and a curious cat,
staring out at the
visitors.

Libby pointed
at one excitedly.
"Kitten!" she
said.

Jacob
laughed as he
looked at the
fluffy cat. "That's
not a kitten, Libby,"
he told her. "That's a big grown-up cat."

"The kittens are kept in the pens
upstairs," Siobhan told them, "but we'll
bring some of them down for you to
meet." She showed them into a lovely
room with a sofa and lots of cat toys. In
one corner there was a huge tower of

scratching posts and platforms for them to climb on. It looked a bit like a playroom, but for cats!

As they waited for Siobhan to come back, Jacob and Libby were so excited they could barely sit still. Libby kept asking if she could climb up the scratching-post climbing frame, but Doug wasn't having any of it!

Natasha perched on the edge of the sofa, her eyes fixed on the door. Any minute now her kitten would come through it!

Siobhan reappeared with a carrying crate containing three wriggling black-and-brown patterned kittens. She took them out of the crate and gave them a cuddle. "Meet Poppy, Peggy and Penny," Siobhan smiled, putting the kittens down.

Natasha giggled. They were so cute!

"They've got lovely markings," Mum commented.

"They're tortoiseshell," Siobhan explained, pulling the door closed. But just as the door was about to shut, another kitten shot in. He was a gorgeous ginger colour, with bright green eyes and fluffy white bits around his eyes and mouth. He tore across the room, then jumped straight onto the sofa, right next to Natasha.

"Oscar, what are you doing here?" Siobhan laughed. "Oscar doesn't belong to the same litter, as you can probably see from his fur."

Oscar jumped up onto the back of the sofa and peered down at Natasha. "Hello, Oscar," she said softly, putting her hand up to stroke his chin. Oscar started purring and nuzzled his head into her hand.

"Oscar's only three months old, but he's already had an eventful life," Siobhan told them. "He was a stray that someone found sleeping outside a fish and chip shop."

Natasha thought about Oscar being on his own and homeless, eating fish and chips from a bin, and her heart melted.

Someone knocked at the door urgently, and then a worried-looking lady poked her head round. "Oh good, you've got him." She smiled in relief. "Naughty Oscar, he ran out between my legs when I opened his pen."

Oscar looked at the new lady, then leaped off the back of the sofa and landed right in Natasha's lap!

"It looks like he wants to stay here!" Siobhan laughed.

"I'll put him back in his pen when the
other kittens go back."

Natasha giggled as Oscar wriggled
around in her lap, then jumped off to go
and explore the cat climbing frame. He
clambered over the other kittens to get
right to the top.

"They're all so sweet!" Mum grinned,
tickling Penny's ears.

Natasha crept over
to the climbing
frame to give
Oscar another
stroke. He
made a funny
chirrupy purr
and flopped
onto his back
to have his
tummy tickled.

Jacob was racing from kitten to kitten, stroking them all. "How are we ever going to choose?" he asked.

Natasha looked at Poppy, Penny and Peggy. They were a bit smaller than Oscar, and they were all incredibly  sweet. Then she looked at Oscar.

"I like Oscar best," she said shyly.

"What do you think, Jacob?" Mum asked.

Jacob shrugged. "I like them all."

"And what do you think, baby?" Mum said to Libby.

"Kitty!" Libby replied.

"It looks like it's up to you, Tash," Doug laughed.

"Oscar, please. Oh please let's get Oscar!" Natasha cried.

"Well, it is going to be mostly yours, so you get the final say," Mum said. "But are you sure?"

Natasha looked at Oscar, who stared up at her, his green eyes wide. He jumped down onto a lower level of the climbing frame, nearly landing on Poppy, who jumped in surprise.

"He seems like a bit of a troublemaker!" Doug chuckled.

Natasha carefully picked Oscar up and looked at his sweet little face. He snuggled into her arms happily and started washing his paws.

*How could anyone abandon you?* Natasha thought. Suddenly she knew that she wanted to make sure he was never cold or afraid or alone again.

"I'm sure," she smiled. This naughty, squirming ball of fluff was *her* cat!

# Welcome Home, Oscar!

Siobhan had explained that someone from Battersea would have to come to their house to check that it was a safe and happy place for him to live, and Natasha was determined to make everything absolutely perfect for when they came. She spent the next few days making the house Oscar-proof.

Doug had helped her set up a

scratching post and some toys to keep
him busy. Natasha had butterflies in her
tummy when the doorbell
finally rang. Doug and
Mum had told her
that it was nothing
to worry about,
but Natasha
couldn't help
it. *What if they
said that she
couldn't have
Oscar after all?*
But she felt a bit
better when she opened the door and saw
the Battersea lady's smiling face.

"Hello," the lady said cheerfully.
Natasha showed her around the house
and pointed out everything she'd set up
for Oscar.

"Mum said he can sleep in my room," Natasha said proudly, crawling under her desk to show the lady the cosy bed she had made for him there.

"This all looks lovely." The lady smiled.

Natasha held her breath. "So . . . can I have him?" she asked nervously.

"Of course!" the Battersea lady said. "You can pick him up whenever you're ready. You weren't worried, were you?"

Natasha nodded shyly.

"I told her not to be," Mum said with a laugh. "But she's a bit of a worrier."

"I just want him to be happy," Natasha told her.

The lady smiled at Natasha. "Oscar is a very lucky little kitten to have such a kind owner. But even a confident kitten like Oscar might be a bit overwhelmed and shy at first. It'll all be very new and a bit scary for him, so don't worry if he isn't very friendly when he arrives.

It doesn't mean he's unhappy, he'll just need a little bit of time to settle down."

Natasha nodded. They'd have all the time in the world because Oscar was going to be hers for ever!

A few days later it was all arranged. Mum and Libby were going back to Battersea to pick up Oscar while Natasha and Jacob were at school. Natasha had chosen a pretty wicker cat basket in the pet shop, and she'd put her favourite blanket in it to make it nice and soft for him. Doug had made sure the basket was secure.

"We don't want Oscar getting out and running all around the car, do we?" he joked.

Natasha didn't know how she was going to wait all day long. She'd never been so excited in her whole entire life. "He's coming today!" she told Megan breathlessly as she rushed into her classroom.

"Ooohhh!" Megan squealed. Natasha had already told her friend all about Oscar's gorgeous orange fur and bright green eyes, and what a special little kitten he was.

"You're so lucky," Megan sighed. "I asked for a kitten for my birthday but Mum said no."

"Yeah, but you're having a cool party!" Gavin said.

Natasha's excitement faded as everyone started talking about Megan's birthday party again.

"I can't wait!" Gavin grinned. "My brother said that when he went, his friend fell off the zip wire and broke his arm!"

Natasha gulped. *Maybe Mum can say I'm ill*, she thought. *Then no one will think I'm a baby for not going.*

When the bell went at the end of the day, Natasha ran out into the playground as fast as she could. Doug and Jacob were waiting for her. "Is he home?" she asked breathlessly.

"Yep," Doug smiled. "He's waiting for you."

Natasha raced home as quickly as she could, breaking out into a run as she overtook Jacob on his skateboard. "Slow down, Tash!" he called.

"I can't," she yelled back at him. "Oscar's waiting!"

"We're up here," Mum called as Natasha burst through the front door. Natasha ran up the stairs, then slowed down as she reached the landing. She didn't want to scare Oscar. "We're in your room," Mum said.

Natasha crept forward on her tiptoes. Mum was sitting on the floor with Libby, looking under Natasha's desk. Natasha knelt down and peered underneath it. Two bright green eyes peered back at her.

Then Oscar leaped
out to meet her.
*Miaow!* he went,
as if he was
saying, "There
you are!" He
padded over
to her and
rubbed his side
against her
knees happily.

"Hello, Oscar!"
Natasha grinned so widely
that her cheeks ached. She couldn't
believe Oscar was actually home!

"Let's take him downstairs and give
him some dinner," Mum said, getting up
and taking Libby's hand.

"Come on, Oscar," Natasha went onto
the landing and called for him.

Oscar trotted out after her, his eyes and ears alert and his tail swishing from side to side as he explored.

"That's the bathroom, and Mum's room, and that's Jacob's room," Natasha told him.

Jacob flung his bedroom door open. "Hi, Oscar," he grinned, bending down to stroke him. "I'm making my room cat-proof."

Natasha stared into Jacob's bedroom. It was even messier than usual. Oscar peered in the doorway, then gave a big jump and leaped over a pile of Jacob's stinky socks, straight onto the bed.

"Look at your room," Mum sighed. "If we lose Oscar in there we'll never find him again."

"He doesn't seem shy or scared at all," Natasha said to Mum as Oscar explored Jacob's room, putting his front paws up on the wall and stretching up to sniff one of Jacob's skateboarding posters, then trotting up the bed towards the window.

Natasha gasped as he put his paws on the windowsill. The window was open!

Without thinking, she jumped over the things on Jacob's floor and grabbed Oscar with both hands. "Jacob, you can't leave the window open," she cried. "Oscar might go outside and get lost!"

"Sorry," Jacob shrugged. "It's not fully cat-proof yet."

"Well, keep your door shut until it is," Mum told him off. "Now, everyone downstairs."

Jacob closed his bedroom door and slid down the banister. Libby bumped down the stairs on her bottom.

Oscar looked up at Natasha and
nudged his head on her chin with a purr.
Natasha felt her heart melt. She kissed
the top of Oscar's furry head. "Welcome
to the mad house," she sighed.

# Oscar the Troublemaker

*CRASH!* That night an enormous noise woke Natasha up. She sat up, confused, and turned on her lamp. Suddenly she remembered – Oscar! She'd played with him all evening then settled the yawning kitten into his bed under her desk.

Now she blinked in the bright light and looked over to his basket. But it was empty. She rubbed her eyes – and stared.

Oscar was sitting at the very top of her bookcase!

"What are you doing up there?" Natasha asked him. There were lots of books on the floor. It must have been the sound of them falling down that had woken her up.

Oscar miaowed and peered down at her. Natasha thought he looked quite pleased with himself to be up so high! The bookcase was so tall she had to kneel on her desk to reach him. She scooped him up in her arms, then carefully climbed down.

Oscar snuggled up to her chest, purring happily.

Natasha carried him back over to her bed and sat down to check he was OK. "You little troublemaker," she yawned. "No more night-time adventures for you!"

She put Oscar back in his basket and then got into bed, pulling the covers up to her chin. But as she turned out the light, she felt Oscar jump up onto the bed next to her. Seconds later he padded round in a circle, purring loudly. Then he curled up and went to sleep.

"Goodnight, Oscar," Natasha whispered happily as she closed her eyes.

That was just the start of Oscar's adventures. He was only a little cat, but he caused a big amount of trouble! The next day Mum came home with lots of shopping bags and Oscar helped 'unpack' them, crawling right inside them and spilling vegetables all over the floor. Then he sat on the laptop when Natasha was working and deleted her homework with his fluffy bum!

"Right, that's it!" Natasha said, after she found Oscar climbing halfway up the lounge curtains. "I'm not letting you out of my sight!"

For the rest of the day, Natasha followed her naughty kitten everywhere to make sure he didn't get into trouble. She spent all afternoon playing with him, wiggling a toy mouse on a string for him to jump on, and he sat on her lap while she had dinner.

When everyone else watched TV that evening, she rolled a ball for him to chase and bat around with his tiny paws.

Eventually Mum said
that Natasha had to
have a bath – and
she couldn't take
Oscar with her.
Natasha felt bad
as she shut the
bathroom door
and Oscar gave
a sad miaow.

"I won't be
long," she told
him. "I can't lick
myself nice and clean
like you can!"

As soon as she was out of the bath and
wrapped in her snuggly dressing gown,
she opened the door. She'd just started
brushing her teeth when Oscar trotted in
to find her.

"Herruw, Ossca!" Natasha said, her mouth full of toothpaste. Oscar bumped his head against her leg to say hello, then started sniffing around the bathroom. He stood on his back paws to peer into the bath, where Natasha's bathwater was draining away, then gave a big jump and nimbly leaped onto the side of the bath.

"Be careful," Natasha warned as the little cat balanced on the narrow ledge, walking along it like he was walking on a tightrope. But Oscar was too interested in the bubbly water. He put out a paw to try and catch some of the bubbles as the water swirled down the drain – and fell in the bath with a splash!

"Oscar!" Natasha cried, rushing over to scoop him out. Oscar gave a startled miaow and scrabbled back out of the bath, his beautiful orange fur flat wet.

"Oh, Oscar!" Natasha couldn't help giggling as she patted him dry with her towel. "What am I going to do with you?"

Oscar miaowed happily. He seemed to have already forgotten about his bath. He just licked his paws, then looked around as if to see what trouble he could get into next.

# Little Cat Lost

On Monday morning, Natasha came down to the kitchen with Oscar trotting at her feet. She was feeling a bit sad that she had school and she wouldn't see Oscar all day long – or be there to stop him getting into trouble.

Libby was leaning out of her chair, reaching down for a piece of toast that she'd dropped on the floor.

"Careful, Libby, you'll fall out," Natasha said. "I'll make you some new toast." As she put a slice of bread in the toaster, Mum came in with a bundle of clean washing.

"Morning, Sugarplum." Mum kissed her on the top of her head. "I'm glad you're up bright and early, because Jacob is going to have to walk you to school today. The car still isn't fixed."

"OK," Natasha agreed as she buttered the toast and gave some to Libby.

"I'm going in five minutes," Jacob yelled from upstairs.

"Wait, I'm not ready yet!" Natasha replied.

"Tough!" he called back, sliding down the banister. Natasha shoved the rest of her toast in her mouth and ran upstairs to get dressed.

She just had time to pull her uniform on and tie her shoes before Jacob started walking out the door.

"Bye Mum, bye Libby, bye Oscar!" Natasha called, hastily zipping up her rucksack and looping it over her arms.

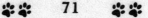

"Wait for me, Jacob!"

Jacob raced ahead, walking on a low wall next to the pavement.

"You'll fall off," Natasha told him.

"No I won't," Jacob replied. "It's fun. You should try it."

Natasha looked at the wall. Oscar would love balancing on it. He climbed on things all the time and *he* didn't hurt himself. Natasha jumped up next to Jacob.

Jacob seemed really surprised.

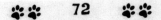

"If Oscar can do it, so can I!" Natasha grinned.

She wobbled a bit as she put one foot in front of the other, but she held her arms out like an aeroplane to steady herself. It *was* fun! She was just getting the hang of it when she heard a familiar *Miaow!* It was so loud it was right in her ear, and it sounded just like Oscar! Natasha turned round so quickly she wobbled and almost fell off the wall.

"Oscar!" she cried.

"What?" asked Jacob.

"Oscar, I thought I heard Oscar!"
Natasha climbed down off the wall and
started looking round.

"Don't be silly, he's back at home with
Mum and Libby," Jacob told her. "Now
come on, or we'll be late."

"I'm sure I heard him," Natasha
whispered to herself.

Jacob stormed ahead, and Natasha had to rush to keep up with him. But every few steps she looked behind her to check for her little cat. She was *sure* that she'd heard him.

She listened hard all the way to school, but she didn't hear another miaow.

Jacob stopped at her school gates. "See you later," he waved.

"Wait, can we call Mum and just check?" Natasha pleaded.

"Stop *worrying*, Tash!" Jacob said crossly. But then he sighed and pulled his mobile out of his pocket. Natasha bit her fingernail anxiously as he called Mum and asked her to check where Oscar was.

"Ask if he's in his basket. Or on my bed, he sometimes likes to sleep there," Natasha prompted her brother. There was a long pause while Mum went to look, and Natasha fidgeted nervously. Then she heard the murmur of Mum's voice on the phone and Jacob frowned, then shook his head.

Natasha gave a shaky gulp as she realized what Mum was saying: Oscar was missing!

# Oscar's Big Adventure

"Now, don't worry," Mum's voice came down the phone after Natasha grabbed it off Jacob. "I'm sure he's absolutely fine, he's just hiding somewhere."

"He's lost, Mum, I'm sure I heard him on the way to school!" Natasha burst out.

"It was probably some other cat, love. I'm sure Oscar's in the house somewhere. Now, why don't you take Jacob's mobile and go on in to school, OK? I'll text you as soon as I find that naughty kitten. Let me talk to Jacob quickly."

Natasha nodded and passed the phone back to her brother.

"OK, OK," Jacob said, hanging up and turning off the phone. He handed it to Natasha. "Don't worry, Tash," he said, "he'll turn up. By the time we get back home he'll be there waiting for us."

Natasha nodded, clutching the mobile tightly. But she wasn't so sure. She'd only taken one step into her bright, sunny classroom before she burst into tears. She just couldn't help thinking that Oscar was out there somewhere, all on his own. Megan and Mrs Coveney rushed over when they saw her face.

"What's wrong, Tash?" Megan asked. Natasha sniffed miserably as she explained.

Megan put her arm round her friend sympathetically. "Don't worry, he took care of himself when he was a stray cat," she reminded her.

Natasha managed a little smile. When she thought about how brave and adventurous Oscar was she felt a bit better.

"He's always getting into trouble and getting out of it again," she sniffed. "But I didn't want him to be on his own ever again." *If only I'd looked after him better*, Natasha thought to herself.

"Now come on," Mrs Coveney said, helping Natasha take off her backpack. "Let's get on with our Maths lesson, and before you know it Mum will be calling to say she's found him safe and sound."

Natasha nodded as she pulled her arms out of the straps. She just wished she knew if the miaow she'd heard *was* Oscar.

*Miaow!* She heard it again, too loud to be in her imagination.

Mrs Coveney and Megan looked shocked. "Did you hear that?" Natasha asked. They both nodded.

Mrs Coveney stared at the bag she was holding. "It sounded like it was coming from—"

"My rucksack!" Natasha cried.

Mrs Coveney put the bag on the table
and Natasha hurriedly unzipped it.
Inside, sitting on her lunchbox, was
Oscar! Natasha picked up the tiny kitten
and hugged him tightly. "Oh, Oscar,
I'm so glad you're OK!" she sobbed.
Oscar gave a deep rumbly
purr in reply.

"He likes getting in bags," Natasha explained to her shocked teacher. "He must have got into my rucksack, and Jacob and I raced out of the house so fast I didn't notice!"

Oscar jumped out of Natasha's arms onto her desk and started looking round excitedly. He seemed to have already forgotten being stuck in the rucksack.

"Look, Tash's got a cat!" Gavin shouted. Suddenly Natasha's whole class clustered around her, all wanting to stroke Oscar.

"OK, first things first," Mrs Coveney clapped her hands. "Megan, shut the classroom door, we don't want Oscar to get lost again, and Natasha, why don't you phone your mum and let her know Oscar's here. I'm very glad he's OK, but I think she might have to come and pick him up. I'm not sure he'd be very good at his times tables!"

Natasha giggled as she dialled her home number. "Mum, Oscar's here!" she burst out when Mum answered. "He's come to school with me in my rucksack!"

"Oh, thank goodness!" Mum sighed.

"That naughty cat! Libby and I will
bring the cat carrier and come and pick
him up."

For the rest of the lesson, the whole
class took turns stroking Oscar as he
jumped from one desk to another.

Everyone was impressed with how daring
he was. No one else's pet had ever come
with them to school before! Natasha felt
proud of her little kitten, who was so tiny
but so brave. Oscar bounded back onto
her desk, and rubbed his soft head
against her chin, purring loudly.

"He's so adventurous!" Megan grinned.

"I just hope he doesn't follow me to the adventure park," Natasha joked.

"Are you coming?" Megan asked, her eyes shining.

"Oh yes," Natasha hugged Oscar close. "If Oscar can have big adventures, so can I!"

# Read on for lots more . . .

🐾 🐾 🐾 🐾

# Battersea Dogs & Cats Home

Battersea Dogs & Cats Home is a charity that aims never to turn away a dog or cat in need of our help. We reunite lost dogs and cats with their owners; when we can't do this, we care for them until new homes can be found for them; and we educate the public about responsible pet ownership. Every year the Home takes in around 9,000 dogs and cats. In addition to the site in southwest London, the Home also has two other centres based at Old Windsor, Berkshire, and Brands Hatch, Kent.

The original site in Holloway

# History

The Temporary Home for Lost and Starving Dogs was originally opened in a stable yard in Holloway in 1860 by Mary Tealby after she found a starving puppy in the street. There was no one to look after him, so she took him home and nursed him back to health. She was so worried about the other dogs wandering the streets that she opened the Temporary Home for Lost and Starving Dogs. The Home was established to help to look after them all and find them new owners.

Sadly Mary Tealby died in 1865, aged sixty-four, and little more is known about her, but her good work was continued. In 1871 the Home moved to its present site in Battersea, and was renamed the Dogs' Home Battersea.

**Some important dates for the Home:**

**1883** – Battersea start taking in cats.

**1914** – 100 sledge dogs are housed at the Hackbridge site, in preparation for Ernest Shackleton's second Antarctic expedition.

**1956** – Queen Elizabeth II becomes patron of the Home.

**2004** – Red the Lurcher's night-time antics become world famous when he is caught on camera regularly escaping from his kennel and liberating his canine chums for midnight feasts.

**2007** – The BBC broadcast *Animal Rescue Live* from the Home for three weeks from mid-July to early August.

# Amy Watson

Amy Watson has been working at Battersea Dogs & Cats Home for eight years and has been the Home's Education Officer for four years. Amy's role means that she regularly visits schools around Battersea's three sites to teach children how to behave and stay safe around dogs and cats, and all about responsible dog and cat ownership. She also regularly features on the Battersea website – www.battersea.org.uk – giving tips and advice on how to train your dog or cat under the "Fun and Learning" section.

On most school visits Amy can take a dog with her, so she is normally accompanied by her beautiful ex-Battersea dog, Hattie. Hattie has been living with Amy for three years and really enjoys meeting new children and helping Amy with her work.

# The process for re-homing a dog or a cat

When a lost dog or cat arrives, Battersea works hard to try to find the animal's owners. If, after seven days, they have not been able to reunite them, the search for a new home can begin.

The Home works hard to find caring, permanent new homes for all the lost and unwanted dogs and cats.

Dogs and cats have their own characters and so staff at the Home will spend time getting to know every dog and cat. This helps decide the type of home the dog or cat needs.

There are three stages of the re-homing process at Battersea Dogs & Cats Home. Battersea's re-homing team wants to find you the perfect pet: sometimes this can

take a while, so please be patient while
we search for your new friend!

**1** Register details

**2** Match

**3** Leaving with your new pet

Have a look at our website:
**http://www.battersea.org.uk/dogs/
rehoming/index.html** for more details!

# "Did you know?" questions about dogs and cats

- Puppies do not open their eyes until they are about two weeks old.

- According to *Guinness World Records*, the smallest living dog is a long-haired Chihuahua called Boo Boo from Kentucky, who is 10.16cm tall.

- Dalmatians, with all those cute black spots, are actually born white.

- The greyhound is the fastest dog on earth. It can reach speeds of up to 45 miles per hour.

- The first living creature sent into space was a female dog named Laika.

- Cats spend 15% of their day grooming themselves and a massive 70% of their day sleeping.

- Cats see six times better in the dark than we do.

- A cat's tail helps it to balance when it is on the move – especially when it is jumping.

- The cat, giraffe and camel are the only animals that walk by moving both their left feet, then both their right feet, when walking.

# Dos and Don'ts of looking after dogs and cats

## Dogs dos and don'ts

### DO

- Be gentle and quiet around dogs at all times – treat them how you would like to be treated.
- Have respect for dogs.

### DON'T

- Sneak up on a dog – you could scare them.
- Tease a dog – it's not fair.
- Stare at a dog – dogs can find this scary.
- Disturb a dog who is sleeping or eating.

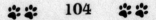

- Assume a dog wants to play with you. Just like you, sometimes they may want to be left alone.
- Approach a dog who is without an owner as you won't know if the dog is friendly or not.

## Cats dos and don'ts

### DO
- Be gentle and quiet around cats at all times.
- Have respect for cats.
- Let a cat approach you in their own time.

### DON'T
- Stare at a cat as they can find this intimidating.

- Tease a cat – it's not fair.
- Disturb a sleeping or eating cat – they may not want attention or to play.
- Assume a cat will always want to play. Like you, sometimes they want to be left alone.

# Some fun pet-themed puzzles!

## What to think about before getting a dog!

Here is a list of things that you need to think about before getting a dog. See if you can find them in the word search and while you look, think why they might be so important. Only look for words written in black. They can be written backwards, diagonally, forwards, up and down, so look carefully and GOOD LUCK!

SIZE
MALE OR FEMALE
AGE
COAT TYPE
COST
BEHAVIOUR
BASIC TRAINING
HOUSE TRAINING
TIME ALONE
GOOD WITH: PETS, CHILDREN, STRANGERS, DOGS
HOW: ENERGETIC, CUDDLY, STRONG WILLED, INDEPENDENT

Remember: when training a dog, reward works better than punishment.

Can you think of any other things? Write them in the spaces below.

107

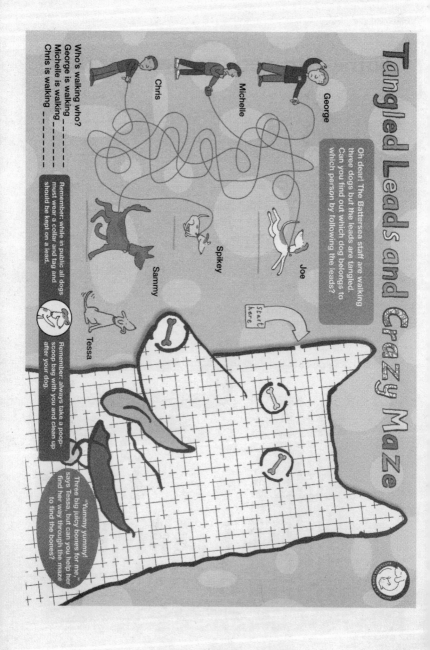

# Tangled Leads and Crazy Maze

Oh dear! The Battersea staff are walking three dogs but the leads are tangled. Can you find out which dog belongs to which person by following the leads?

Chris

Michelle

George

Spikey

Joe

Sammy

Tessa

start here

**Who's walking who?**
George is walking _ _ _ _ _ _ _
Michelle is walking _ _ _ _ _ _ _
Chris is walking _ _ _ _ _ _ _

Remember, while in public all dogs must wear a collar and tag and should be kept on a lead.

Remember, always take a poop-scoop bag with you and clean up after your dog.

"Yummy yummy! Three big juicy bones for me." says Tessa, but can you help her find her way through the maze to find the bones?

# Drawing dogs and cats

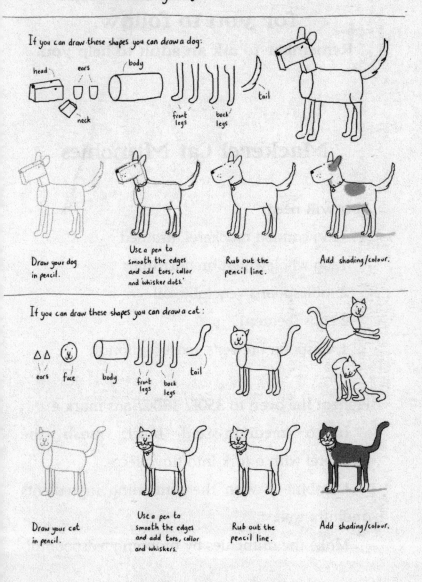

If you can draw these shapes you can draw a dog:

head
ears
neck
body
front legs
back legs
tail

Draw your dog in pencil.

Use a pen to smooth the edges and add toes, collar and 'whisker dots.'

Rub out the pencil line.

Add shading/colour.

If you can draw these shapes you can draw a cat:

ears
face
body
front legs
back legs
tail

Draw your cat in pencil.

Use a pen to smooth the edges and add toes, collar and whiskers.

Rub out the pencil line.

Add shading/colour.

# Here is a delicious recipe for you to follow.

**Remember to ask an adult to help you.**

## Mackerel Cat Munchies

**You will need:**

115g canned mackerel, drained

120g wholewheat breadcrumbs

2 tablespoons vegetable oil

2 eggs (beaten)

1 teaspoon brewer's yeast (optional)

Preheat the oven to 350F/ 180C/ gas mark 4.

In a medium-sized bowl, mash the mackerel with a fork into tiny pieces.

Combine it with the remaining ingredients and mix well.

Make the munchies by dropping teaspoonful-sized dollops of the mixture onto a greased baking tray.

Bake for 8 minutes.

Once cooked, remove from the oven and cool to room temperature, then store in an airtight container in the fridge.

There are lots of fun things on the
website, including an online quiz, e-cards,
colouring sheets and recipes for making
dog and cat treats.

# www.battersea.org.uk